To Scott —
Be a team player!

Robert Skead

ELVES CAN'T KICK

Robert Skead, Elves Can't Kick

ISBN 1-929478-66-6

Published by

Cross Training Publishing
317 West Second Street
Grand Island, NE 68801
(308) 384-5762

Tale Blazer Productions
371 Butternut Avenue
Wyckoff, NJ 07481

Library of Congress Cataloging in Publication Data in Progress.

This book belongs to:

_____

Age: _____

School: _____

Favorite Soccer Player(s):

_____

_____

_____

Favorite Soccer Team(s):

_____

_____

_____

For my favorite goalkeepers
TH and PG:
Thanks for being such
great friends!

"Soccer? It's the beautiful game."
Pele

Also By Robert Skead:

ELVES CAN'T DUNK tells the story of Sebastian, a young basketball fan who decides to tryout for his favorite professional basketball team. Only there is a small problem —Sebastian is an elf and ELVES CAN'T DUNK. To solve his dunking dilemma, Sebastian takes some of Santa's special feed corn, the stuff that makes the reindeer fly, and heads for the tryout. This corn will give Sebastian more hang time than Michael Jordan on the moon! When Coach Frank Tanner finds out about the corn, he sets out on a mission to steal it from Santa Claus. Soon, its up to Sebastian and his friends Ralphy the polar bear, Holly the elf and Santa himself to catch Coach Tanner and save Christmas!

ELVES CAN'T TACKLE -- Sebastian is back in this sequel to *Elves Can't Dunk*. Only now, Sebastian and the gang are on a mission to give Jack Fabulous, professional football's most famous quarterback, a little Christmas spirit. In the process, Sebastian ends up on the team for the big Christmas Eve Day "Sandwich Bowl" game—only there is a large problem, Sebastian is an elf—and ELVES CAN'T TACKLE! The book delivers good news about the true meaning of Christmas and the importance of loyalty between friends.

HITTING GLORY - A BASEBALL BAT ADVEN-
TURE is the heartwarming story about Lou Gibson, an
eleven-year old boy who finds an old wooden baseball bat
in his school's basement. When Lou recalls that the most
famous graduate of his school, Public School #132 in New
York City, was Yankee great Lou Gehrig, he immediately
sets off on a mission to prove that the bat once belonged
to "The Pride of the Yankees." Lou's search sends him on a
journey of triumph, tragedy and discovery.

SAFE AT HOME—A BASEBALL CARD MYS-
TERY tells the story of Trevor Mitchell, an 11-year-old
boy, whose aged great-grandfather gives him a 1915 Babe
Ruth rookie card valued at $50,000. Trevor's joy is threat-
ened by the mysterious disappearance of the card and by
his friends' skepticism about great-grandpa's claim of being
the only man in baseball history to steal home off Babe
Ruth.

Contents

CHAPTER ONE
Game On

The fresh coat of springtime snow at Santa's North Pole headquarters crunched with each soldier-like step made by Ralphy the polar bear during his morning security patrol. When he saw something strange blowing in the distance, Ralphy's eyes flashed with curiosity and he sprang into action. He sprinted toward the fence that protected Santa's village. Ralphy slowly approached a piece of ripped, tan fabric, grabbed hold of it with his paw, and looked at it closely, his expression filled with concern. "Sebastian! Come here!"

Nearby, Sebastian, wearing a red ski jacket and a hat decorated with reindeer watched six seals passing a red kickball to and fro with their noses. He marveled at how the ball never touched the ice. He ran toward Ralphy. "What is it?" he asked.

"It's not good! Look!" Ralphy handed the woolen fabric to his two-foot eleven-inch tall elf friend.

Sebastian's eyes widened. The initials BH were embroidered on the scarf.

"Bertha Hayworth," said Ralphy.

Sebastian met Ralphy's eyes. "Or maybe Coach Bud Hill."

Sebastian took a deep breath. For months, Bertha Hayworth, the cooking and craft queen of the United States, had threatened to steal Mrs. Claus's recipes and to tell the world the whereabouts of Santa's secret North Pole workshop. Sebastian figured she was jealous of Mrs. Claus's success in the Christmas treats business.

Bud Hill coached the Boca Del Vista Elks professional football team. After seeing Ralphy's talent on the football field, he had said that he'd like to go to the North Pole and sign all the polar bears to professional football contracts. The polar bears couldn't possibly play in the NFL because not all the stadiums are air-conditioned.

"Either way, there's trouble," said Sebastian.

A gust of cold wind blew across the compound. Snowflakes fell all around them. The brown scarf flapped in Sebastian's hand.

Then, in the distance, an alarm sounded.

"That's coming from Santa's workshop!" exclaimed Sebastian. He gave Ralphy a worried look, but Ralphy had jumped into action by plopping down on his stomach and starting to slide on the snow. Sebastian ran up to him and leapt onto his back as if Ralphy were a sled. The two belly slid as fast as they could toward Santa's headquarters.

Moments later, they arrived at Santa's headquarters and darted inside.

Sebastian covered his sensitive elf ears with his red-gloved hands to block the sound of the blaring alarm. Ralphy sprinted right behind him.

Inside Santa's family room, elves scurried frantically.

"WHERE'S SANTA AND HOLLY?" Sebastian yelled, over the alarm.

Just then, Mrs. Claus bolted into the room. "THEY'RE GONE! THEY'RE GONE!"

At that moment, the alarm stopped.

"WHO'S GONE?" yelled Ralphy. He noticed the quiet. "Sorry."

"Not who? What!" replied Mrs. Claus. "My recipes!"

Bertha Hayworth has been here, Sebastian thought, *and only moments ago. She must have tripped our alarm and gotten away.* He gazed at the "BH" on the scarf in his hand. "It's Big Bertha! And she can't be far away!" Sebastian's voice echoed through the silence.

"We got that loud and clear, good buddy," said Ralphy, his ears still ringing.

"My recipe for Polar Bear Claus Paws, and Secret Snowdrop Surprise with white chocolate, and all my other recipes... I...I... I can't believe she did this," said Mrs. Claus. A tear ran down her rosy cheek. "Look! That jealous Bertha left me a nasty note and an empty plastic film container."

"She's a litterer too!" said Ralphy, shocked.

Mrs. Claus held up a piece of notepaper decorated with lovely spring flowers. She read it out loud. "I've got your recipes. I win. I always do. Now, I must run. This alarm is giving me a slight headache. By the way, you should buy my book, *Bertha's Chic Interior Design.* Your house is way overdone with the rustic-holiday motif! Ta! Love, Bertha." Mrs. Claus paused. "She can't use my recipes. I have special ingredients available only here at the North Pole. If she uses anything else people could get sick."

"Oh no!" said Ralphy.

"Attention all elves! Attention all elves!" a voice exclaimed over the loudspeaker. It was Holly, the Chief of Security. "Big Bertha has just been spotted on the east side of the village. Drop everything! Pursue and capture!"

"Thank goodness!" said Mrs. Claus.

"Come on! Let's go!" shouted Sebastian. He dashed out of the room with Ralphy and the elves close behind.

Outside, Bertha Hayworth plodded through the deep North Pole snow in her expensive black designer boots. Bertha's quick steps generated *loud* crunching noises thanks to her plump, muscular body. Her red hair blew gently from under her fur-trimmed winter hat. Large puffs of foggy steam blew out of her mouth and she tried to catch her breath. Bertha heard the alarm stop. Her escape route had been carefully planned and she was almost where she wanted to be. She dove behind a woodshed, like a skilled soldier, and hid herself. She then raised her head carefully and searched her surroundings for any sign of the enemy.

Santa's village was peaceful and quiet, except for the honking of a flock of snow geese flying in the cold, gray sky. Bertha patted the chest of her parka with her hand, double-checking that Mrs. Claus's recipes were still safely in her possession.

They were. She smiled happily. Bertha stood up, ready to make her next move.

"Freeze, Chubby," said a tiny, squeaky voice. It was Wilson, the North Pole's tiniest elf, who stood only two feet tall. His candy-cane-striped jacket bundled him warmly. "Turn around slowly and keep your hands where I can see them."

Bertha slowly turned around and laughed in her deep, scratchy cackle.

A short distance away, Holly, Sebastian, Ralphy, and a team of elves and security polar bears maneuvered themselves into the area. They hid behind snow banks and trees.

"I see her. There she is." Holly peered through her binoculars. She brushed her strawberry blonde hair from her eyes, aimed her binoculars down and noticed Wilson. "Oh no!" Holly jumped to her feet. "Be careful, Wilson!"

Bertha turned and saw Holly.

"You elves don't scare me!" shouted Bertha.

The elves and polar bears started to move toward Bertha.

"Wait!" shouted Holly. "We don't want her to hurt Wilson."

Everyone halted.

Wilson cleared his throat. "This is the X25," said Wilson. "The most powerful squirt gun the North Pole has ever made. Only, I can't remember if it's loaded or not. So I ask you…. are you feeling lucky?"

"Silly elf," Bertha chuckled. "You can't shoot water at me. It's practically below zero degrees out here. That water will freeze before it even hits me."

Bertha took a step toward the tiny elf.

Wilson squeezed the trigger and a spray of thick purple slime shot from the gun and hit Bertha right in the face.

"Oooow! What is this? Get this off me!" she cried.

"It's jelly!" said Wilson.

In the background, the elves and polar bears laughed in delight.

The jelly dripped onto her coat. Bertha took out a hanky and quickly wiped her face. "You rotten misfit!" said

Bertha, angrily. "You stained my $2,000 jacket!" She reached down to grab Wilson. Just then, a snowball pounded her in the head.

"Good shot," said Ralphy to a grinning Sebastian.

Bertha reached for Wilson again.

A polar bear threw another snowball that hit her in the arm.

Wilson laughed.

Anger filled Bertha's eyes, and, in a quick motion, she struck like a snake, caught Wilson and dropkicked him into the air.

The elves watched Wilson soar over their heads and sail right through an open barn door behind them.

"Goal one for me," Bertha said. She threw her arms into the air in celebration.

"That's it, Bertha. Now, you've got us mad!" shouted Holly.

Bertha turned her attention to Holly. Suddenly, she saw 100 snowballs coming right at her. The machine-gun like barrage of snow forced Bertha into cover behind the woodshed.

Bertha, the elves and polar bears exchanged round after round of snowballs in the most intense snowball fight the North Pole had ever seen. Bertha wanted to fulfill her plan and escape, but at the same time she seemed to enjoy the combat. The elves and polar bears chased after Bertha, but she maneuvered herself into new positions, using much of Santa's compound as the battlefield.

While the battle was raging, Santa arrived on the scene with Spalding, the North Pole's top inventor.

"Santa!" exclaimed Sebastian, as a snowball zoomed past his face. "What took you so long?"

"I had to comfort Mrs. Claus. She's not used to naughty people," Santa said. "And I had to help Spalding with this."

Santa stepped aside, revealing a red and green cylinder that looked like a cannon.

"I never thought I'd ever have to use it, but I can see she is very resourceful and athletic. In fact, she is at the top of my Naughty list!" said Santa.

Bertha was using ice balls like baseballs and batting them with her rolling pin.

"This is a heat-seeking, laser targeted enemy catcher," said Spalding. "It shoots a net. Watch."

Spalding activated the unit just as a snowball nailed him in the face.

Bertha's grizzly laugh echoed in the distance.

Spalding carefully removed the snow from his half-moon glasses. He pointed the device in Bertha's direction.

"Heat-seeking sensor activated." He flicked another switch. "Laser beam on." He adjusted the blaster.

"Huh? What's that?" Bertha looked down and noticed a red laser beam light on her jacket. She glanced in the distance and saw Santa and the device. Bertha bolted as fast as she could in the opposite direction.

"Fire," said Santa.

KA-BOOM!

The machine fired a ball made of ropes through the air.

Bertha ran in a zig zag pattern. She looked over her shoulder and her mouth fell open wide.

The ropes flew in all directions as they chased her.

She changed directions. The ropes formed a net and followed her every move.

A heartbeat later, the net engulfed her and she fell to the ground.

BAM!

The elves cheered. Sebastian high-fived Spalding and Ralphy. "Way to go, guys!" he shouted.

Santa shook his head in disappointment. "I wish it didn't have to come to this."

Holly and the gang marched toward Bertha, who sprang free from the net holding a pizza cutter in her hand.

"You can't catch the craft queen! I have more gadgets than James Bond and let's see—they all have my logo on them. How nice for me!" Bertha did a sort of jig.

"All right Bertha, so you're crafty," said Sebastian. "Return the recipes and maybe you'll actually get a present from Santa for Christmas. Besides, you can't use those recipes." He explained about the special ingredients. Sebastian searched for some way to capture Bertha.

"Yeah, right!" shouted Bertha. "Like I believe that!" She examined her surroundings. She was close to where she wanted to be.

Ralphy motioned to his polar bear security team to get ready. He looked at Santa for approval. When Santa nodded, they sprang into action. They charged at Bertha like a wall of linebackers going for the tackle.

Bertha watched the polar bears rushing at her.

The bears leapt into the air for the tackle.

But so did Bertha! She jumped high into the air like a ballerina filled with helium.

The bears hit nothing but air and then the ground. They slid like out-of-control bowling balls into the distance.

Bertha laughed. She scurried ten feet ahead to a warehouse building, with Sebastian, Holly and the gang running after her.

Bertha opened a Christmas sack filled with soccer balls and kicked them expertly at her targets. One after another, she knocked down Sebastian, Holly and every elf who came after her.

"Score! Score! Score!" yelled Bertha. "You'll never get these recipes back!"

Santa and Spalding watched in disbelief.

Bertha kicked the last soccer ball and looked to her left. She grinned. Her teeth twinkled in the North Pole sunlight. Now, she was right where she wanted to be. Her snowmobile was parked next to the warehouse. She jumped on it and started the engine.

"Later, elf people!" She drove it in a circle around them, teasing them. Elves and polar bears tried to chase after her, but she eluded them each time.

"Ta-Ta, Santa baby!" exclaimed Bertha. "By the way, you're too pale to keep wearing red. Try pastels!" She then aimed her snowmobile in the opposite direction and headed for the passage out of Santa's secret valley.

"How did she find out about the valley?" asked Holly.

"Come on, gang!" Sebastian yelled.

The rest of the elves ran with him to the stable. Sebastian planned to use the reindeer and sleighs to catch Bertha. He knew an assault from the air would bring success.

When the team ran into the stable their mouths fell wide open in horror. Santa's sleigh had been dismantled. The runners were removed and broken. The reindeer had gags around their mouths so they couldn't make a sound. Rope had been tied to their antlers, connecting them with super duper knots. Strange-looking locks had been put on their stall doors. Even Santa's jet powered sleigh, the Nick-

Crusier, had been taken apart—pieces of it were scattered across the dirt floor.

Santa entered, looked over the situation and shook his head sadly. He and Spalding started to help the reindeer.

Sebastian, Holly, and Ralphy hung their heads. "What do we do now?" asked Sebastian.

Holly shrugged with despair. "I don't know."

CHAPTER TWO
Team Meeting

Toward the eastern end of Santa's village, Spalding's laboratory was filled with state-of-the-art electronics, gadgetry and science equipment. All of his greatest ideas became reality there. Spalding and Santa had gathered Mrs. Claus, the elves, and the polar bear security team together for a special meeting. Sad faces filled the room.

Mrs. Claus's recipes were the secret of her success. They had been in her family for generations. Millions of people around the world enjoyed her tasty Christmas fruitcakes, cookies and treats.

"The secret for success, on any mission, is to know your opponent," Spalding said confidently, sounding like a government agent. "We gathered you here so I could share with you some information about Bertha Hayworth."

"You mean Big Bertha!" said Holly.

Santa gave Holly a look.

"Sorry," said Holly.

Sebastian winked at her.

Santa cleared his throat. "Here's what we know about

Ms. Hayworth," he said. "As you know, Bertha was not a Nice little girl. She made the top of our Naughty list five years in a row."

Santa hit his remote control and the lights dimmed. A picture of Bertha as a child appeared on a large viewer screen.

"She talked back to her mom and dad," said Santa.

An image appeared on the screen of Bertha with her hands on her hips making a whiney face.

"She wouldn't clean up her own messes."

An image appeared of Bertha shaking her head "no" at a messy kitchen table piled high with crayons, tape and papers.

"She whined about what her mom had prepared for dinner. She lied when she got in trouble. And she stole chocolate from the kitchen cupboard, when her mother told her she couldn't have any more treats. This was little Bertha's daily routine when she was a child." Santa showed a picture of Bertha with a face covered with chocolate.

Even though the elves were accustomed to hearing about children's bad behavior, they gasped in disbelief.

"As you also know, Bertha grew up to be one mean and nasty adult," Santa continued. "However, deep down I know she has the potential for goodness. She lives in New York City, also known as The Big Apple, where she has a cooking and crafting empire. Her cooking business is Number 2 in the market, second to my wife's successful operation." Santa blew his wife a kiss.

"Bertha's business is hurting and so is her personal wealth. She is spending more than she is making. It seems she is addicted to buying and collecting things, especially picture frames. She has them by the thousands everywhere."

"She probably has a picture of herself in each frame," Sebastian said softly to Ralphy.

"Yuck!" Ralphy winced.

Santa continued. "Big Bertha, I mean Bertha... also owns a professional soccer team."

Sebastian snapped to attention.

"Her soccer team is losing money because of its losing streak, year after year." Santa hit his remote and an image of the team appeared on the screen.

Spalding took the center stage. "The name of her team is the New York Blenders. My research also reveals that Bertha was quite an athlete in her younger days."

"No kidding," said Holly, under her breath.

"She was the star soccer player on her high school and college teams," added Spalding. "She loves soccer even today, which is why she still keeps the Blenders, even though the team is losing money."

Santa flicked the remote control off and the lights came on. "Bertha has also threatened to reveal our secret location if we try to stop her from using Mrs. Claus's recipes, but that's a chance I'm willing to take. I've decided to send a few of you to New York to try to get them back. Perhaps at the same time you can teach Bertha that stealing is wrong."

Sebastian's mind flashed back to his last adventure with the Boca Del Vista Elks football team. *It's practically springtime in New York,* he thought to himself. *At least it won't be hot like Florida.*

Santa walked up to Holly. "As my Chief of Security, I want you to go and lead the team."

"I'll do my best, Santa."

"Ralphy, you're strong and fast. Holly will need you to deal with Bertha. I'm holding you responsible for her safety."

"I'm your bear, Santa. You can count on me," said Ralphy.

Santa stopped for a moment to think.

Sebastian's head dropped.

"Don't worry, Sebastian. You're going too." Santa smiled.

"You had me worried for a second," said Sebastian.

"You should be worried," added Santa, seriously. "Even though New York is the greatest city in the world, it is still a tough place." He paused. "As soon as Spalding repairs the NickCruiser, you'll be on your way. Rest assured, you'll be in our thoughts and prayers."

"Thank you, Santa. Don't worry, Mrs. C. We'll do our best for you," said Holly.

"I know you will," said Mrs. Claus. "Just promise me you'll be careful."

"We will," said Sebastian. "Look out Big Apple and Big Bertha! Here we come!" Sebastian gave Holly and Ralphy a high five.

CHAPTER THREE
Road Trip

The New York City skyline with its tall skyscrapers decorated the horizon. It reminded Sebastian of thousands of picture postcards Santa received throughout the year.

While they flew overhead, Sebastian and Ralphy marveled at the sight of Central Park. Never did they imagine there would be so much open land, grass, trees and water in the middle of a big city.

"Hey, look! The trees are starting to grow leaves!" Sebastian pointed.

"And the flowers are starting to bloom!" said Holly.

Ralphy was thankful that there was still a chill in the air.

Moments later, Holly landed the NickCruiser on top of New York's most famous toy store—Kamler's, which was located near the park. The team found their way to the street and headed for Bertha's office building. People walked rapidly around them.

"This is so much busier than Polarville," said Sebastian.

"Tell me about it," replied Ralphy, feeling a bit overwhelmed.

Holly couldn't help but gaze up at the tall buildings. They seemed to reach up to heaven itself.

HONK! HONK! BEEP! BEEP!

Sebastian, Holly and Ralphy could feel the excitement of New York City in the air while they walked quickly, like everyone else around them.

"Spalding said to go to Park Avenue," said Holly, looking down at her map, then up again at the street sign in front of her. "Here we are. Big Bertha's lair should be right across the street."

Sebastian gazed at the sign on the building. "Hayworth Enterprises," Sebastian read out loud.

During much of the flight to New York, the team had discussed how to get the recipes back. Santa had reminded them that they couldn't do anything illegal or immoral to get them back. Breaking in and stealing them would be unacceptable. With that in mind, they decided to take the direct approach—they would simply go to Bertha's office, request a meeting and ask for the recipes to be returned.

The team entered the Hayworth Enterprises building and Holly marched up to the security desk.

"We're here to see Bertha Hayworth, please," said Holly. She winked at Sebastian.

"Name?" asked the female security guard.

"Holly. I'm in the security biz too."

"Oh really? Holly what?" The guard looked at Ralphy and Sebastian curiously.

"No last name. Just Holly. This is Sebastian and Ralphy."

"Do you have an appointment?"

"No."

The security guard laughed.

"What's so funny?" said Sebastian.

"If you were me, would you let you in?" the woman asked Holly.

"Well, knowing me, I'd say yes, but I see your point. We really need to see Big Bertha... Oops, I mean Bertha." Holly winced.

The security guard laughed louder—only now she couldn't stop herself.

Holly and Sebastian exchanged looks, but the guard kept laughing.

"You... want to see... one of the most famous women in New York... without... an appointment?" The guard controlled her laughter. "Now, that's funny." She wiped a tear from her cheek. "Why would Ms. Hayworth want to see you?"

"Actually, she wouldn't," replied Ralphy. "We recently bombarded her with snowballs."

The guard snapped her fingers and three other security guards approached the desk. Seconds later, Sebastian, Holly, then Ralphy found themselves spinning out of the building's revolving glass doors. They landed on the sidewalk on their bottoms.

"Sorry, guys," said Ralphy, rubbing his sore posterior. "I guess I shouldn't have mentioned the snowball thing."

Sebastian stared up at the building. "Well, the Queen of Crafts is in there somewhere," he said.

"No she's not," replied Ralphy.

"What do you mean?" asked Sebastian, still gazing upwards, mesmerized by the tower of steel and glass.

"She just got into that long, black car," said Ralphy.

Sebastian and Holly turned to look. They saw Bertha's plump bottom enter a stretch limousine, followed by her legs and feet. Sebastian noticed that Bertha had on a pair of designer sneakers.

"That's the mean redhead, all right," Ralphy nodded.

"Come on! Let's follow her!" Holly dragged them by the arm.

They ran to Kamler's Toy Store and, in seconds, the NickCruiser was in the air over Fifth Avenue.

Inside the long, black limousine, Bertha Hayworth stretched her legs and dialed her cell phone.

"Vincent darling, yes, I'm off to the stadium now to meet with that goalie gentleman, Paul Howard. You know, the one who's also in cooking school and keeps sending me ideas? If he'd just stick to the goalie business maybe we'd win a game! Seems the lad is also quite intelligent and studied archeology in college, specializing in deciphering ancient writing. Maybe he can make sense out of some of this awful handwriting and these strange ingredients." Bertha took a moment to admire herself in a hand-held mirror. "Anyhow, in case he is unsuccessful, I want you to chemically analyze all the ingredients in every one of Mrs. Claus's products and replicate them for me. I'll get to the bottom of her recipes one way or another. Got that?… Good. Now, be a good chemist and do that for me, dear or *I'll fire* you before you can say cookie dough!"

Bertha turned her cell phone off. She clicked a button causing the glass between her and the driver to glide open.

"Drive faster, Hobson. Time is money, after all!"

In the sky above, Holly piloted the NickCruiser as fast as she could. Sebastian and Ralphy looked down at the city streets and searched for the long, black car. Unfortunately, the streets were filled with vehicles that looked just like Bertha's.

"There it is!" exclaimed Ralphy, excitedly. "Two blocks to the left!"

"How do you know?" asked Holly.

"Her logo is on the roof," replied Ralphy.

Sebastian saw Bertha's cooking logo on the roof of her car. "At least that makes her easy to find," he chuckled.

In the distance, Holly noticed the soccer stadium. "I bet that's where she's headed!" shouted Holly.

"Bertha's stuck in traffic. Let's speed ahead of her and get there first," said Sebastian.

Holly put the NickCruiser into high gear and they headed for the stadium.

Within moments, they arrived. Sebastian read the sign on the wall of the soccer arena. "Hayworth Stadium. Home of the New York Blenders."

Holly looked for a safe place to land where they wouldn't be noticed and to hide the jet-powered sleigh.

"Spalding told me that the team is known throughout the league as the team that Bertha's ego built," said Holly. "They also have the best looking uniforms—designed by Big B herself."

Sebastian wanted to laugh, but he was too busy thinking of a plan. *Big Bertha needs the recipes because her business is failing,* thought Sebastian. *That means she won't need the recipes if her business is successful.* "That's it!" shouted Sebastian. "If we help Bertha make money, she won't need the recipes. Maybe then she'll give them back!"

"We can't help her beat Mrs. Claus's cooking business," said Ralphy. "That wouldn't be right."

"True," said Sebastian. "But what if we help her soccer team to win? Then they will make money. Spalding told us her first love is soccer. A winning team could make more money than her other businesses!"

"I don't believe I'm saying this," said Ralphy. "But I think you're onto something here."

"Any better ideas?" Sebastian asked Holly.

Holly shook her head and landed the NickCruiser.

The three friends carefully entered the stadium and hid near the stands. They watched the New York Blenders practice taking shots on goal. On another part of the field, some players played a mini-game with cones as goals. Sebastian was impressed with the skill of the athletes. He loved basketball and dabbled in football, but he had never played on a soccer team. He figured he had enough exposure to professional sports (thanks to his last two adventures) to offer the team advice on how to win. It didn't take him long to leave his two friends and walk up to the coach.

"Excuse me, sir." Sebastian gazed up at the coach.

The balding, blonde-haired coach turned to see who addressed him. He saw no one until he looked down at tiny Sebastian.

"Um, my name is Sebastian. And I was wondering if I could get out there and kick the ball around with your team."

The coach's eyes lit up. "Sebastian? Sebastian, you say?"

"Yes."

"There is only one player I know who uses only one name. And that is Sebastian from the famous Manchester team."

"But um..."

"You are much shorter than I imagined..."

"I'm..."

"Yes, Sebastian yes! Feel free to kick the ball with my team. It would be an honor."

The ball was put into play and it bounced to Sebastian.

Instinctively, Sebastian dribbled the ball down the field—only not with his feet—with his hands!

The players all yelled at him.

"Oops," said Sebastian. "Sorry."

The practice continued. The ball went from player to player on offense. Sebastian noticed that a few of the men hogged the ball and didn't pass it to an open man when they should have.

Soon, the ball once again came to Sebastian. He tried to stop it with his foot as he had seen the others do, but the ball knocked him over. He got up and ran after it, filled with determination. He went for the kick and MISSED the ball entirely!

"Elves can't kick," said Ralphy, from his position hiding in the stands.

Holly nodded.

"You are *not* the Sebastian from Manchester!" screamed the coach. "Get off my field, you imposter!"

Sebastian walked off the field with his head low.

"Don't feel bad, little fella," said Paul Howard, the Blenders' goalkeeper. "He yells at me a lot too. Maybe you're just in the wrong position. I hate to run. That's why I'm a goalie."

Sebastian gave Paul a half-hearted smile. "Thanks, Mr. Goalie." He walked over to Holly and Ralphy.

"Nice try, Sebastian." Holly hugged him.

"Soccer definitely isn't for me either, pal. I want to grab that ball, and run with it for a touchdown," admitted Ralphy.

"I kicked a soccer ball once," said Holly. "And it hurt my big toe."

"Hey, I like what that goalie guy said. Maybe I can play

goalie!" Sebastian raised his head, excited about his idea.

Just then, he saw Big Bertha walk onto the field. "Get down! Hide!"

Bertha walked briskly onto the field. The practice came to a screeching halt.

Bertha walked right up to Paul Howard. "Mr. Howard."

"Why so formal? You can call me Paul. Though you usually refer to me as 'the guy I'm paying too much money to' or 'the guy who keeps letting too many goals in' or 'loser,'" Paul said, removing his goalie gloves from his hands.

"Well, you know those sports reporters, they're always misquoting me." Bertha batted her long, fake eyelashes at Paul. "I understand you actually graduated from college, studied archeology, and are very talented at deciphering unknown languages."

"You've read about me on the team's Web site," answered Paul, his thick, sweaty, black hair glistened in the sun. "I'm also single," he joked.

Bertha hesitated for a moment. Was the goalie flirting with her? "I, um, knew that as well. I know everything about all my employees." Bertha pulled out Mrs. Claus's recipes from her jacket. "I need your help. I want you to help me make sense of these. The handwriting is quite awful. I can't read it, even with my own brand of designer reading glasses."

"She has the recipes with her!" Sebastian exclaimed, hiding in the stands. He wanted to run down and grab them.

Paul carefully took the old papers and read them. "Recipes," he said.

"Yes," replied Bertha. "Can you make out every word?

There are twelve that are giving me trouble, twelve important words," she blurted out, impatiently.

"Whose recipes are these?" asked Paul.

"A friend of mine gave them to me," replied Bertha. It was hard to lie when looking into Paul's blue eyes.

"It might take some time, but I believe I could decipher these words. By the way, did you receive the ideas and recipes *I* sent you?" Paul paused. "Tell you what... I'll help you if you help me."

Bertha paused. "Women are much better chefs than men, you should..."

"Excuse me! I'm sure this is an important meeting, but we're running a pre-game warm up here." It was the coach. His tone was polite, but firm. "We have a big game today against our biggest rival."

"Yes, I know. The Norfolk Torpedoes," said Bertha.

"Seems I remember reading they don't like you very much," said the coach. "Isn't that the team that has a life-size cardboard cutout image of you in their locker room?"

"Yes. They use it for target practice. I'm told its part of the rivalry. It would be nice to beat those guys... for once." She leered at the coach.

"Well, you're paying me to coach these men, remember? Let me do my job."

Bertha's mouth curled in a half smile. "Oh, I'm sorry. Is that what you were doing? But what do I know about soccer? You may continue." She grabbed the recipes from Paul. "I'll be in touch... handsome." She turned on her heels to walk away, and noticed elf ears and Ralphy's white fur sticking up from the stands. There was also a police officer behind them. Bertha turned and gestured for the coach to hand her the ball. "May I?"

The coach handed her the ball, but dropped it just before she could take it.

The ball bounced once in front of Bertha. She flicked the ball expertly up into the air with her toe, kneed it, then spun around in a circle like a karate expert and booted the ball across the field and into the net!

Everyone on and off the field was wide-eyed with amazement.

"She's unbelievable," said Ralphy, peeking from behind a seat.

"Tell me about it," said Sebastian.

"She's still just as naughty. Don't forget it, boys," added Holly. "Let's get those recipes."

"Eh-hem." The police officer put his thumbs in his belt and cleared his throat behind them.

Sebastian turned around. "Oh, hello, Mr. Officer, sir," he said.

Bertha skipped off the field. "I see the Clauses didn't take my threat seriously," she said to herself. "They sent spies with the *police* to arrest me. I'll teach them that they need to take my threats seriously. They'll be plenty busy with unwanted visitors when I get done with them."

She ran down the tunnel of the stadium, looking behind her to see if she was being followed. Then, she took out her cell phone and pressed a button that connected her immediately with her office. "Rose, darling," Bertha said to her assistant, mustering her charm. "Be a doll and send that map of the North Pole I showed you to the *New York Gazette,* with a note that I discovered the secret location of Santa's Headquarters." A pause. "Yes, I am serious." A pause. "No, I don't want to take a vacation! And who cares if they think I'm crazy? As long as they print it and spell my name right. Do it now or I will *fire you* faster than you can say Ho Ho Ho! Thank you, doll." Bertha hung up and placed her cell phone in her jacket.

Bertha walked past the equipment room with the recipes held firmly in her hand. "They won't be able to arrest me. I'll hide the evidence," she said to herself. She stopped dead in her tracks, conceiving an idea. She darted into the equipment room. She looked left, then right, for a place to hide the recipes. She smiled, opened her jacket, and took out a small pocketknife with her logo on it. Racks filled with soccer balls stood in front of her. Bertha picked up a soccer ball and opened a section of the leather cover with her knife. She carefully placed the recipes between the ball's inside bladder and its leather covering. Her deep-scratchy laugh echoed throughout the room.

Near the field, the police officer escorted Sebastian, Holly and Ralphy out of the stands.

"We can get passes, sir. Just give me some time," said Sebastian.

"I hear that from kids just like you sneaking in every game," replied the policeman. His navy blue uniform, patches, and holster reminded Sebastian to respect those in authority.

"Hey, these…" It was Paul Howard, the goalkeeper. He struggled for a word. "… um… *people* are OK. You can let them go." Paul ran up to them.

"You know these characters?" the officer asked.

"Yes, they are my guests," said Paul. He picked up Sebastian. "I'll get them the appropriate passes. I'm sorry for the confusion."

The officer mumbled something under his breath and left.

"Thanks," said Sebastian to Paul.

"No problem." Paul put Sebastian down. "My family couldn't make it to the game today. You can have their passes. Here." Paul handed the passes to Sebastian.

"This is awesome! How come you're doing this for us?" asked Sebastian, while he admired the Blenders logo on his special VIP pass.

"I'm told one of my gifts is being able to tell who's good. You three are good eggs. I can tell. Enjoy the game."

"I don't mean to be rude, but we have a mission to fulfill," added Holly. "Remember, BH—the reason we are here. The pieces of paper we have to get back."

"That's right," said Sebastian. "We'll catch you later, Mr. Goalie. Come on, team."

Before Sebastian could run, Holly had grabbed him and Ralphy by the arms. They headed in the direction Bertha had gone.

In the equipment room, Bertha sat on a stool. She expertly stitched the leather ball back together with a needle and thread. She then found a pump, put the perfect amount of air inside the ball, and kissed it. Bertha dropped the ball and juggled it a few times with her foot. Then, her cell phone rang to the tune of "Hey, Good Looking. What you got cooking?" Bertha placed the ball on a rack, which held dozens of other identical soccer balls.

"The lovely Ms. Hayworth here. Um, yes, my dear, overpaid chemist. Did you figure out Mrs. Claus's ingredients yet, so we can replicate them?" A pause. "What? You can't figure out some of the ingredients in her Polar Bear Claus Paws? Ok. Use substitute ingredients and make some. Bring a batch to me here at the stadium pronto." She hung up her phone.

Suddenly, the door flew open.

"Hello Bertha." It was Sebastian.

"That's *Big* Bertha," added Holly, with a grin, as she stepped beside him.

"I'm not big. I'm big-boned," replied Bertha. She looked at her reflection in a nearby window.

"I have to tell you—*you* have a great arm. I've never seen a woman throw snowballs like you did," said Ralphy.

"Yes, well, I do everything well," Bertha replied.

"You know why we're here. We want the recipes," said Holly, firmly.

"I don't have the recipes. You can search me," said Bertha. She held her muscular arms open. "I have nothing to hide."

"We saw you with them a few minutes ago," said Sebastian. "You are very naughty. Give them back. They are the property of Mrs. Claus. You stole them. Stealing is wrong!"

"And how did you know about Santa's secret valley passage? No one knows about that," said Holly with her hands on her hips.

Bertha laughed. "Oh that! That valley passageway is almost impossible to see because of its zig zag shape. It looks like an ice wall, but Captain Don Adams told me what to look for and I drew a map based on our conversation."

"You know about him?" said Holly.

"Crazy Captain Don? The Mighty Explorer of the North," said Bertha. "Of course I know him."

"Who's Crazy Captain Don?" asked Ralphy.

"The only man to find Santa's secret valley passage that leads to our village," answered Holly.

"It seems no one believed poor Don when he returned

to civilization years and years ago," said Bertha. "No one, that is, except for me. I heard about the legend and the crazy coot and found him. It was worth a shot talking to the old timer. I'd say it paid off."

"Well, you got what you wanted, but stealing still isn't right. Give the recipes back, please," said Sebastian. "They belong to Mrs. Claus, not you."

"You love Santa's wife. I can tell," said Bertha.

"Yes, we do," said Holly. "She is very good."

"Known her for a long time, I suppose." Bertha glanced at the soccer ball that held the recipes.

"All our lives," replied Sebastian.

"When she writes you a note for your birthday or Christmas, can you always read her handwriting?"

"Every word," said Holly.

Bertha drummed her fingers on the special soccer ball. "Mrs. Claus sent me a letter once."

"She did?" said Sebastian.

"Yes. Only I can't read all of it. Can you help me read just 12 words? I'll have my assistant show you each word. It bothers me that I can't read what that sweet, old woman wrote to me. I'm so sad." A manufactured tear ran down Bertha's face.

"Ah, don't cry, please," said Ralphy. "I can't stand to see anyone cry. Let's help her."

"I don't believe her," said Holly. "Give us back the recipes and then we'll help you read the letter, if there really is one."

"Holly's right. Give back the recipes," said Sebastian. "You can't use them. We told you—if you do, people will get sick."

"Nice try, little elf," replied Bertha.

"Mrs. C has special ingredients found only at the North Pole," said Sebastian. "Besides, you can't bake like Mrs. Claus. No one can. She uses melted Christmas snow for water, that's what makes everything taste so good. Her elves help her make the flour. Our tiny hands knead the dough just right."

"I could hire short people to make flour," said Bertha, liking the idea.

"In addition to her secret ingredients, Mrs. Claus puts goodness and love into everything she bakes. That's why what comes out of her oven makes her Number 1." Sebastian winked at Holly and Ralphy.

Bertha started to breath heavily. Her face turned red as an apple.

"You all right, lady?" asked Ralphy, nervously.

"Did. You. Say. Number. One?" Bertha's neck veins bulged. "I hate being Number 2!" she blurted out. "You can't have the recipes back! I'm Number 1 in crafts. I'm number 1 in decorating! I'm Number 1 in publishing! I'm Number 1 in TV shows! I'm Number 1 in everything, except cooking! Thanks to Mrs. Claus, I'm Number 2!"

"Your soccer team is in last place," said Sebastian, softly.

Bertha jerked her head at Sebastian. She looked like she was going to grab him the way she'd grabbed Wilson, but just then the door flew open.

"Excuse me. Almost game time." It was the equipment manager. "Can't have a soccer game without soccer balls." He brushed everyone aside and took hold of the rack of soccer balls. He wheeled it out of the room.

Bertha lunged to stop him, but quickly stopped, not wanting to look suspicious. She noticed the police officer walking by the open door.

"I'll make a deal with you," said Sebastian. "You want

those recipes to help you be Number 1. But you can make more money with a winning soccer team than in all your other businesses combined. Here's my offer. If I help your team win, you give back the recipes."

Bertha laughed. "You think you can make that bunch of losers win?"

"Yep," said Sebastian, confidently.

"You sure you can do that?" whispered Ralphy.

Sebastian nudged him with his elbow.

"You've never won a game against the Torpedoes, have you?" asked Holly.

"No," replied Bertha, in an annoyed tone of voice. Bertha looked torn, as if she were calculating options. "If I make this deal will you leave me alone for a while?"

"Yes," said Sebastian.

"Fine. You get my Bad News Blenders to beat the Torpedoes and I'll give you back your precious recipes," Bertha lied. She stuck out her hand.

Sebastian smiled and shook it.

That is one sweaty and clammy hand, thought Sebastian.

CHAPTER FOUR

The Match

Sebastian sat in the stands and gazed at all the empty seats in amazement. *Every single one of these seats could be filled if this team was winning,* Sebastian thought to himself. He glanced at the Blenders, dressed in purple and white-striped uniforms. The Blender logo was stitched over the left chest and depicted a blender with soccer balls exploding out of the top. On the front of the jersey was a larger image of the Hayworth Enterprises company logo.

The public address announcer welcomed the 4,000 fans to Hayworth Stadium, which could hold up to 50,000 people. He then introduced the opposing team—the Norfolk Torpedoes. High-energy music filled the arena. The New York Blenders jogged onto the field to screams, cheers and applause, which echoed in the nearly empty stands.

Each player held an autographed soccer ball in his hand. After the National Anthem was sung, each player kicked a ball into the stands, to the fans' delight.

The Blender fans held up signs that read, "The Blenders Are Going to Mash You Up!" and "Go Blenders!"

Sebastian locked eyes with Paul Howard, who wore number "18." Paul jumped up and down and stretched. He gave Sebastian the "thumbs up."

Bertha led Sebastian, Holly and Ralphy to the team's bench. She saw Paul with his thumb in the air and thought he was gesturing to her. She raised her thumb to him in return. Paul's teammates watched in horror.

"Tommy baby." Bertha marched up to the coach. "You're fired. Go take a shower."

The coach's mouth dropped open. "What? You can't do this! I have a contract!"

"You violated that contract when you ate at a non Bertha Hayworth franchise two months ago," said Bertha "I know eating a burger and fries is hardly worth losing your job over, but rules are rules, and I made the rules. Ta-Ta, Baldy."

Sebastian tugged on Bertha's jacket. "You didn't have to do that!"

Bertha ignored Sebastian. "Men, I want to introduce you to your new coach. This is…" Bertha looked down.

"Sebastian."

"This is Sebastian," Bertha continued. "I see the refs want to start the game, so listen to him." Bertha spotted the bags of soccer balls and headed for them.

"Um. Hi." Sebastian gazed up at his new team. In front of him was Joe Batto, a strong stopper from Africa. Next to him was Clint Jolley, the team's leading scorer. Nelson Perez stood next to Clint and played center forward.

Sebastian didn't have time to get to know everyone. The refs blew the whistle signaling for the game to start. *Good thing they have their names on the back of their jerseys,* Sebastian thought. "Starting team, get out there!" Sebastian shouted. "Let's hustle and score some goals!"

"That was brilliant," said Bertha sarcastically, while she closely examined a soccer ball.

The Blenders ran onto the field. Once the ball was put into play, the Norfolk Torpedoes took immediate control.

"Let's go, soccer people!" exclaimed Ralphy, from the bench area.

"Amazing. I can't believe we're actually cheering for Big Bertha's team," said Holly, standing beside him.

In the broadcast booth, the announcer, Chip Chapin, did the play-by-play. "The Torpedoes are dribbling with some fancy footwork out there, as the Blenders scramble for the ball. Oh! And it's Jolley with the steal! Jolley takes control of the ball, Joe Batto is wide open, but Jolley keeps the ball… The ball is stolen by Steve Shak of the Torpedoes! He evades the Blender defense, has a clear 25-yard shot at the goal. Shoots… and SCORES! Paul Howard made a high-flying dive, but could not get to it in time."

"Nice try, Paul!" shouted Sebastian.

Paul got up, brushed himself off, and kicked the ground in frustration.

Sebastian perused the row of players on the bench. He spotted Bertha shaking a soccer ball by her ear. Bertha quickly placed the ball back in the bag when she saw Sebastian watching her. She walked away.

As the first half of the game continued, Sebastian studied his team carefully. The concept of scoring in soccer was no different than in basketball or football. And the principles of teamwork were the same. He noticed that Clint Jolley and Nelson Perez never passed the ball. He also saw that many of the players didn't want to help one another on the field.

This team has a morale problem, Sebastian thought to himself.

Sebastian cheered on his team and was amazed at how fast 40 minutes went by. He glanced up at the scoreboard. There were only five minutes left to play in the first half. The score was 4 to 0, and the Blenders were not winning.

"Those recipes have to be somewhere in the stadium. Bertha had them moments before we found her," Holly told Ralphy. "You keep an eye on Big B. I'm going to use this pass and snoop around."

"Bertha isn't moving far from those balls," said Ralphy. "I won't take my eyes off her."

Holly headed for the equipment room. She searched every inch of it for the recipes, and she found nothing. She then searched every nook and cranny of the underground of the stadium. Still no recipes—only dust and old candy wrappers.

The players entered the tunnel for the half time break.

Sebastian walked past Holly and they exchanged nervous looks.

Clint Jolley kicked open the door to the players' locker room.

"We can come back and win this thing!" said Sebastian, following his team.

"Little dude, we can't win," said Nelson Perez. "Our coach gets fired moments before the game. We get you, someone who can't even kick a ball and who obviously doesn't know a thing about soccer. We can't play in these conditions. I'd quit if I could, but that Bertha writes a contract that is as tight as a submarine."

"And she pays us peanuts!" said Clint.

Bertha entered the room, followed by Ralphy.

"Did I hear someone say peanuts?" asked Ralphy.

"How many of you guys like Christmas?" asked Sebastian.

Everyone raised his hand.

"Winning at sports is just like Christmas," said Sebastian. He paced the room. "Winning is about teamwork. It's about giving and sharing. And you know what happens when you share the ball?"

"What?" the room said in unison.

"You share an opportunity. And you share in a win!" Sebastian pointed at Clint. "Mr. Jolley. You know, I like your name. I like jolly people."

"Doesn't everyone?" said Clint.

"I'll be a whole lot jollier, and so will these fans, when you share the ball with Nelson when he is open. And Nelson you do the same," said Sebastian. "The two of you could be a powerful one two scoring machine if only you'd pass the ball. You'll each have more goals at the end of the year if you pass it to one another. I promise."

"Oh, isn't this sweet," said Bertha. "Sharing time."

Sebastian pointed his finger at Bertha. "You! I want you out of my locker room!" shouted Sebastian. "Ralphy, escort Ms. Hayworth out, please."

Ralphy gave Bertha a bear hug and lifted her out of the room. Bertha tried to speak but Ralphy placed his paw over her mouth.

While they exited the room, Ralphy let her go. Bertha huffed and turned to go back inside the locker room when the equipment manager drove by with another bag of balls. Bertha followed the bag like a hungry cat following a mouse. Ralphy trailed her like a private detective.

Inside the locker room, the men couldn't believe what their eyes had just seen. They waited for Bertha to bolt back into the room, but it didn't happen.

Sebastian explained to the team that he was from a far

away place and that he had watched seals in the North play a game similar to soccer. He told them about the seals' ability to move the ball from player to player without having the ball touching the ground.

Sebastian drew a trick play on the chalkboard. "Use your heads out there, team. Think about those seals! Let's win this game. More than you can imagine is resting on it, but let's win it for each other! Don't let your mean owner steal your joy and love for this game!" Sebastian clapped his tiny hands. "Let's get out there and sink those Torpedoes!"

The team stood silent for a moment. Then, like a volcano erupting, they cheered and dashed out of the locker room in a roar of excitement.

CHAPTER FIVE
Between the Pipes

The second half of the game started.

The Blenders had four goals to score in order to tie the match. Bertha left the bags of balls and marched up to Sebastian.

"No one talks to me that way, little shrimp."

"I'm sorry, Bertha," said Sebastian. "Please forgive me."

Bertha didn't know how to react. "Um, don't let it happen again."

All around them, cheers rose from the stands. Bertha and Sebastian quickly looked at the opposing team's goalie. Clint Jolley had just scored on a beautiful crossover pass from Nelson Perez.

"Yes!" cheered Bertha, caught up in the moment.

Sebastian looked at Bertha curiously.

The score was now Torpedoes: 4, Blenders: 1.

The game continued. Sebastian was a quick learner. He was amazed at how the men could run forever.

On the field, Joe Batto trapped the ball with his chest. The ball dropped to the ground. The Torpedo defense rushed into the ball's path. Joe stayed with the ball and avoided a steal. Another Torpedo player charged up like a raging bull. Before Joe could get off a pass, Joe's opponent accidentally kicked him hard in the ankle. Joe tumbled to the ground in pain.

"Oh no!" shouted Sebastian.

The refs stopped the game while the team's trainer went to Joe's side. A stretcher was brought out and some men carried Joe off the field.

Sebastian studied his bench. Then it hit him... *Would she?* he thought. "Bertha!"

"What?" replied Bertha, feeling one of the soccer balls for any sign of the hidden recipes. "I'm not doing anything wrong!"

"I hear from a good source that you were a great soccer player."

"Still am. I'm good at everything."

"Get in the game," said Sebastian.

"But coach, what about us?" grumbled the players seated on the bench.

"I can't play. This is... a men's league," said Bertha, hating every word.

"Well, if you can't compete with the boys..." Sebastian perused his bench for another player to put in the game.

"What! You know I can!" She marched in front of Sebastian.

"Is there a written law that says a woman can't play on the team?" asked Sebastian.

"No." Bertha lied. She walked up to Jim Regan, the tallest guy on the team, who was seated on the bench. "You, Smiley Guy, number 29, give me your jersey."

Regan quickly took off his jersey and gave it to Bertha. She put it on. She approached Sebastian.

"You silly little elf. Don't you realize I can make this team lose? You'll never get the recipes back now." She jogged onto the field.

"What are you doing?" shouted Holly, from the sidelines. She ran up to Sebastian.

"Bertha's competitive nature is stronger than her greed," Sebastian told Holly.

"Are you crazy?" exclaimed Holly.

"Trust me," Sebastian replied. "Let's go, Blenders!" yelled Sebastian and clapped his hands.

Holly shook her head and jogged back to the sidelines.

Bertha stood out like a sore thumb on the field. Not only was she was a woman, but she wore long pants.

"It looks like Bertha Hayworth, the Blenders' owner, is now on the field, as a PLAYER!" said Chip Chapin, from the broadcast booth. "I know this is the Blender's biggest rivalry, but this woman will do anything to grab a headline. And there she goes right for the ball. Oh my... I don't believe my eyes. Bertha can run! She runs like a deer! Bertha steals the ball, dribbles past the defense through a maze of legs... Oh! She hammers a kick and SCORES! Bertha Hayworth has just scored her first professional soccer goal! And it is obvious the men on the Torpedoes didn't like it one bit!"

Bertha ran back to her position and high-fived a few of her teammates.

Sebastian gazed at the scoreboard, which read Torpedoes - 4, and the Blenders - 2.

Everyone on the field, the bench and in the stands was amazed.

"That Bertha Hayworth has one strong leg on her," Chip stated.

"Way to go, 29!" shouted Paul Howard, from his goal.

Bertha turned to Sebastian. "That was just to prove I could do it!" She ran down the field.

Ralphy walked up to Sebastian. "Neither of us know much about soccer, but are you sure you know what you're doing? Take her out of the game, pal. She's naughty, not nice."

A smile formed on Sebastian's face. "But look at her. She is so competitive," said Sebastian.

Bertha jolted after the ball and stole it. She kicked the ball ahead of herself like a seasoned veteran. The defense closed in on her. Bertha booted the ball back and forth from foot to foot, passed it to the open Clint Jolley, who maneuvered the ball down the field. Clint passed it back to Bertha.

"Go Big B!" shouted Sebastian.

Holly watched in amazement.

Bertha fired a long, curling shot and put the ball between the pipes for a goal!

"That's 4 to 3!" shouted Holly.

Bertha celebrated with a back handspring. She ran to the stands and rejoiced with the fans who chanted her name: "Bertha! Bertha! Bertha!"

"That was one amazing pass from Clint Jolley to the incredible Bertha Hayworth. Is there anything this woman can't do?" Chip Chapin loosened his tie and poured himself a glass of water.

Sebastian wondered if Santa and the gang were watching this game on TV. He realized he had a lot of explaining to do when they returned. *I just hope we return with those recipes,* Sebastian thought. He chuckled and he watched Bertha raising her arms, pumping up the crowd with excitement.

50

The men on the Norfolk Torpedoes steamed in anger. They brought the ball downfield quickly and skillfully. The Blenders' defense bore down on the ball, but Steve Shak faked the defense. Seconds later, Shak was in range for a shot at Paul Howard and the goal. Shak positioned himself inside the box near the mouth of the goal. He booted the ball at the upper right corner of the net.

Paul Howard leapt and deflected the ball!

THUD! CRASH!

"Oh no!" Chip Chapin exclaimed. "Howard is down! He hit the goalpost hard! I think he's knocked out cold!"

Bertha ran to attend to Paul. So did the trainer and the rest of the team. Sebastian, Holly and Ralphy followed behind.

Bertha knelt down on one knee. She leaned over the unconscious goalie and slapped his face gently. "Paul. Paul. Wake up. Oh my… Please." Her voice cracked full of emotion. She ran her fingers through his thick hair.

The trainer pushed Bertha aside. He took out smelling salts and placed it under Paul's nose. Paul's eyes immediately opened in surprise—and pain.

"Ow. My head. What happened?" said Paul, with a dizzy and disoriented haze.

"You crashed into the goal post," said Sebastian.

"For the fifth time in your career," said Clint, shaking his head.

"I hate it when that happens," said Paul. He rubbed the large lump on his skull.

Bertha pushed the trainer out of the way. "Are you all right?"

"Yes. Um. Well, yeah. I think so… Beautiful," replied Paul.

"Beautiful? Someone get an ambulance! I think he scrambled his brain," said Clint Jolley.

Paul tried to stand to his feet, but his knees gave way and he collapsed.

"He's in no condition to play," said the trainer to everyone.

Sebastian gazed at his team, who were all standing by their injured teammate. He looked for another player wearing a goalie jersey. "Where's the backup goalie?" asked Sebastian.

"He hurt his big toe. He's at home resting," said Joe Batto.

"Who else plays goalie?" Sebastian looked for a volunteer.

"I was the goalie for the Happy Time Preschool," said Jim Regan. "But that was a few years ago."

Paul tried to stand on his feet again. Bertha grabbed him by the hand and helped him up. As Paul balanced himself, his eyes met Bertha's squarely. "You have beautiful eyes," he told her.

Bertha blushed.

"Get him to a doctor fast!" yelled Clint.

The trainer helped Paul hobble off the field.

Bertha pointed at Sebastian. "You! You're the new goalie!"

"Me?"

"Yes, you."

Paul took off his goalie gloves and threw them to Sebastian. "Here. These will help."

Sebastian held up the gloves, which were ten sizes too big. "They won't help me." Sebastian happened to be standing in the center of the goal. He slowly looked up, then to his left and right. The area between the pipes seemed vast to him. "I can't play goalie!"

"Just keep the ball from going in the goal," shouted Paul, while he was escorted off the field.

"That helps a lot," Sebastian said softly to himself. He wished he had some of Santa's special feed corn that makes the reindeer fly. *At least then I'd be able to jump,* thought Sebastian.

CHAPTER SIX
The Game Continues

Sebastian stood in the center of the goal. Before he had time to even think, the referees started the game again.

A Blender player threw the ball in to Nelson Perez, who worked the ball down the field. Nelson passed the ball to Bertha, who tapped the ball over to Clint, who flipped the ball back to Bertha.

Within moments, Bertha evaded everyone. The only thing that stood between her and the goal was the goal-keeper. Bertha's mouth curled in a half-smile. She faked left with the ball, and launched her shot. The ball took off from her foot like a missile and curved over the diving goalie and into the back of the net!

"That was for you, Paul," she said to herself.

The score was tied 4 to 4.

"All right, Big B!" shouted Sebastian. He clapped his hands.

The opposing team put the ball into play. They started to boot the ball to one another. Before Sebastian knew it, they were running right toward him at midfield. Sebastian's eyes grew wide. *Oh no.* What do I do? Sebastian thought. He fastened his eyes on the ball. *Stop the ball. Stop the ball.* Sebastian bounced on the balls of his feet. His defense raced after the ball, which was now at the feet of the famous Steve Shak. Sebastian's heart beat like a drum.

Shak took a shot on goal that zoomed through the air like a line drive.

Sebastian launched himself for the save, but it was as if he were rooted to the ground.

The ball sailed by Sebastian's hands and smashed into the net!

"And the Torpedoes take the lead again five to four on an easy goal for Steve Shak," said Chip Chapin, in the broadcast booth. "My grandmother could score on that pint-sized goalkeeper, or coach, or whatever he is."

Sebastian rose to his feet. "This isn't fair!" he told Bertha. "What happens if we tie?

Bertha responded with her grizzly cackle. "Those recipes are mine, little elf," Bertha said in a voice that only Sebastian could hear. She glanced at Paul on the sidelines. "I hope he's well enough to decipher those recipes for me," she said softly.

Sebastian picked the ball up off the ground and kicked it angrily. Only the ball didn't go forward. It sailed behind his head and into the stands.

"Elves can't kick," repeated Ralphy. He quickly picked out a *new* ball from the bag and threw it onto the field.

"Come on Sebastian!" cheered Holly, while the opposing team put the ball into play.

Suddenly, the ball began wobbling as it rolled around on the field. The Torpedo player dribbling it could not control it.

The ball rolled as if it had a mind of its own. Bertha watched from her position. Her heart raced and she took off for the ball like a rocket.

The ball rolled uncontrollably.

Wobble. Wobble. Wobble.

Bertha sprinted to gain control of the ball. She dribbled confidently. Her eye aimed on setting up a shot.

Wobble. Kick. Wobble. Wobble. Stumble. Kick. Wobble. Wobble. Trip.

"What's wrong with this ball?" shouted Bertha to herself. She tried her best to maneuver it within shooting range.

Sebastian, Chip Chapin, and all the fans, watched curiously.

Bertha pulled back her leg for the shot. "The recipes!" her voice echoed through the arena and her foot collided with the ball-

BOOM! POP!

The ball whistled through the air like a popped balloon.

The deflating piece of black and white leather soared in every direction and toward the Torpedo goal.

The goalie dove after it like he was trying to catch a flying whoopee cushion.

It zoomed past him and gently landed against the net.

"Yes!" shouted Bertha.

Recipes floated in the air around them, blowing to and fro in the gentle spring wind.

Sebastian, Holly and Ralphy sprang into action.

"And the Blenders tie the game on another miraculous goal by Bertha Hayworth," said Chip. He took off his tie and poured himself another drink of water.

A recipe floated in the air in front of Clint Jolley, who

swiped it. "Claus Family Christmas Fruitcake," read Clint. He studied the old piece of paper curiously.

"Those are mine!" shouted Bertha, and she ran and jumped, trying to grab as many of the recipes blowing in the wind as possible. She had six in her clammy hands.

The referee and two other Torpedo players held most of the recipes. One remaining recipe blew softly like a feather in the wind. Sebastian and Bertha ran after it like two outfielders going after the same fly ball.

While Bertha lunged in the air to catch it, Sebastian ran up her leg, then her back and arm and grabbed it with his tiny elf hand. Legs still pumping, his momentum took him flying into the air.

THUD!

He hit the ground hard.

Bertha quickly sprinted and stole the recipes from the referee and players' grasps. She headed for Sebastian.

"What's going on here? We have a soccer game to play!" exclaimed the referee.

Bertha jammed on her brakes in front of the referee. "There seems to have been a defective ball. We're just cleaning up," said Bertha in her sweetest voice. "We don't want litter on the field," said Bertha. She then stomped up to Sebastian. "Give me that piece of paper, little goalie, or else!"

"No!"

"We have a game to play. The refs are waiting."

"No. Give me back those recipes. They aren't yours! They belong to…"

Bertha grabbed Sebastian and placed her hand over his mouth.

"Leave him alone!" demanded Holly and Ralphy.

Bertha easily took the recipe from Sebastian. She gently placed him on the ground, patted him on the head, and smiled warmly at him. Bertha then skipped over to Jim Regan, the tallest player on the team. She presented Jim with all the pieces of paper in her hands. "Be a doll and hold these. Give them back to me after the game and I'll give you a large cash bonus."

Jim's eyes lit up. "I'll hold 'em. Don't worry." He carefully refolded them and placed them inside his pants pocket.

"Soccer is a continuous game, Ms. Hayworth." The ref held up a yellow card in the air.

"Oh, and Bertha Hayworth gets her first yellow!" said Chip Chapin, in the broadcast booth.

Sebastian gazed up at Bertha with disappointed eyes. "You'll never truly be Number 1," said Sebastian. He shook his head. "In your heart, you'll always know you aren't because you have to lie and steal to get there. Cheaters may prosper, but they don't sleep well at night."

Bertha gazed up at the scoreboard. "The score is tied, little guy. There's only one minute left to play. Our deal only gave you *the goods* back if we win. We never mentioned a tie. And there's no way we're going to win because there's no way I'm going to help you."

Sebastian anchored his gaze at the scoreboard. His heart sank for a moment.

"Did you just say you're not going to help us?" asked Clint.

Bertha didn't answer.

Sebastian watched the other players and refs run down field to resume play. His mind raced for a solution. "Regan! Get in the game for number 33!"

Jim Regan quickly put on another player's jersey and ran onto the field.

Bertha jogged back into position.

"This game is starting!" The referee presented the ball to a Torpedo player, who threw the ball into play.

Sebastian's eyes flashed bright. A smile jumped to his face. "Let's go, Blenders. We can win this thing. Remember that play I drew for you! Think of the seals! Think of the seals!" Sebastian clapped his hands. He looked at the clock. Fifty seconds remained in the game.

"Seals?" said Bertha to herself curiously.

The Torpedoes booted the ball down the field.

Clint Jolley swooped down on the ball and intercepted it. He paused and looked at Sebastian out of the corner of his eye. He flicked the ball up with his foot and headed the ball like a seal to Nelson Perez, who headed it back to Clint, who headed it to Jim Regan, who headed it back to Nelson. The three passed the ball back and forth to each other in the air, almost supernaturally! Whenever it looked like the ball might be stolen, they passed it to the tall Jim Regan, who headed the ball easily without interference.

"Go! Go! Go!" shouted Holly and Ralphy.

In the mouth of the goal, Sebastian barked like a seal and laughed.

"No one can get the ball away from Jolley, Perez and the rest of the Blenders!" shouted Chip Chapin into his microphone. "Why, they look like a bunch of seals out there! They are running circles around the opposition!"

Bertha stopped in her tracks. Her mouth dropped open and she watched the ball move gracefully down toward the goal without ever touching the ground.

On the bench, Paul Howard rubbed his eyes. "Are those seals out there?" asked the dizzy goalie.

On the field, Bertha took off like a rocket toward Nelson Perez.

"Oh, no!" said Sebastian.

In the broadcast booth, Chip Chapin rose to his feet. "And there goes Bertha. But what is she doing? She's not positioning herself for a pass. She's running at Nelson Perez like she wants to hurt him!"

Not knowing what was happening behind him, Clint Jolley headed the ball toward Nelson. The ball went high in the air. Two Torpedo players jumped up to stop the pass, but missed. Nelson thrusted his skull forward to head the ball.

"Look out!" exclaimed Chip, practically covering his eyes.

Nelson and Bertha's heads collided with the ball.

PING! PING!

The ball went back and forth between Bertha and Nelson's heads over and over again like a pinball machine.

The teammates fell to the ground.

THUD! UMPH!

The soccer ball floated in the air like it was in slow motion. A Torpedo player readied himself to receive the ball. Near the goal, Clint Jolley positioned himself for the pass. The scoreboard clock counted down: 8, 7...

Suddenly, Nelson Perez jolted to his feet and launched his body into the air. His head slammed into the ball like a hammer, before Bertha could grab his foot.

The ball cut its way through the air.

Everyone in the stands rose to their feet.

"And there's the header pass to Jolley... Clint Jolley leaps and heads the ball and SCORES! GOOOOOOOOAL! The Blenders win! The Blenders win!" Chip Chapin danced in the broadcast booth. "What amazing teamwork! I've never seen anything like that in all my years in soccer! This could be a great season for the

New York Blenders. I've never seen head passing like that! These guys look like they were trained at Sea World! Stick around for my post game report, which is brought to you by Bertha's Bagels, the ah… best tasting bagel in New York."

The bench cleared. Everyone ran toward Clint and embraced. Sebastian, Holly and Ralphy joined the pile of celebrating players and jumped on top of them.

On a quiet corner of the field, Bertha huffed and puffed in anger. She glared at the site of triumph. "You can't do this to me," she said to herself, staring at Sebastian.

Sebastian gave Clint a high five. "Nice shot, Jolley."

"Thanks, coach."

"That was the best passing I've ever seen," said Sebastian to his men.

"We used our heads and shared, coach!" they exclaimed.

Sebastian turned his focus to Bertha, who was still huffing. He walked up to her.

Holly, Ralphy and the team followed.

"A deal's a deal." Sebastian stuck out his hand. "We won. Now, may we please have the recipes back?"

Bertha jumped to her feet. "No way!"

"You promised. You gave your word," said Sebastian.

"That doesn't matter," replied Bertha. "These losers can't win again."

"We did. We can. And we will," said Clint. "You just wait and see."

"That's right!" said Joe Batto. "We're a team."

Bertha walked up to Jim Regan. "I'll take back those papers now. I'll have my assistant give you the money. You'll have it before you leave the stadium."

"Don't give them to her. They're ours!" said Holly.

"Give them to me, Mr. Regan. I'll even make sure you start next game," said Bertha and she stuck out her hand.

Jim ran to the bench and got his warm up jacket. He jogged back to Bertha and took the papers out of his pocket. He began to read: "Five sticks of butter. One cup Whale blubber."

"You can read that?" Bertha exclaimed. "Whale blubber?"

"My father's a doctor," said Jim. "His hand writing is atrocious. Reading unreadable handwriting is my specialty."

Bertha's grin grew ear to ear. "I'm going to make you very rich, Mr. Regan." Bertha practically drooled with excitement. "Give me the papers, please. Now!"

"Don't do it, dude," said Clint.

Bertha held out her hand. She smiled warmly at Jim and the rest of the team. "That was a great game. You know, you guys all deserve more money. I'm going to give bonuses to all of you." She fastened her eyes on Jim. "The papers."

Jim looked at Sebastian, whose eyes told him it was ok. Jim turned his attention to Bertha. "You're the boss," Jim said. He placed the recipes in her hands.

"Good. Now, all the players get bonuses. And now you can give those recipes back to us, so we can give them back to Mrs. C," said Sebastian, with his hand extended toward Bertha.

"Yeah, we need to get home," said Ralphy.

"Hand them over, Bertha. I'm losing my elf-patience," added Holly, with her arms crossed.

Bertha held the recipes close to her chest. "No. Have a nice trip home—empty handed."

"Oh, Ms. Hayworth! Ms. Hayworth! I have them! I have them!" called a voice from a man running onto the field. It was her food chemist, Mr. Flavor. He wore a lab coat and a chef's hat. "I brought the special batch of Polar Bear Claus Paws just like you wanted. I got here as fast as I could."

He stopped at her feet, and presented a tin of treats.

"Special batch?" said Paul, excitedly. He reached in and grabbed a treat.

"No!" shouted Sebastian, Holly and Ralphy, in unison.

But Paul had already taken a huge bite.

"What's the big deal?" asked Bertha.

"You replicated the recipe, didn't you?" asked Sebastian.

"Of course I did," replied Bertha.

Paul grabbed his stomach and buckled over in pain. He groaned and moaned. Red spots formed on his face.

"What's happening to him?" asked Clint.

"What's wrong?" asked Bertha.

"We told you," said Holly. "That stuff will make people sick. That's why we're here."

Paul moaned.

"Oh, my! Look at his face," said Bertha. "Help him!"

There was silence. No one knew what to do.

Paul curled up on the ground. He groaned loudly.

Bertha knelt by his side. "I'm sorry. I didn't know."

"I think I know what can help!" Sebastian took off and ran to the NickCruiser. He opened a cooler in the back and took out a bottle of sparkling, carbonated North Pole water. He quickly ran back to the field with it. "Here," he said, bending down and holding it at Paul's mouth.

Paul took a slow sip, then gulped it down.

"Mrs. Claus always gives this to me when I have an

upset stomach," said Sebastian. "It's special North Pole Christmas water."

Within moments, Paul began to feel better and the red rash began to disappear from his face.

"Hooray!" shouted Holly.

"Good thinking, little buddy," said Ralphy with a high five.

"Thank you," said Paul. "My stomach feels better, but my head is still ringing."

"We'll take those recipes back now, please." Holly stuck out her hand.

"No way. Mr. Regan can read these," answered Bertha with a smile.

"Bertha, that's not right," said Paul.

There was a long pause while their eyes connected.

"Oh, come on. I bet I can even get the right ingredients from the North Pole."

"You don't need the recipes," pleaded Sebastian. "You have a winning team now."

Bertha gazed at the Blender players, then at Paul, whose face had turned light green.

Clint placed his arm around Paul. "Man, we have to get you to a hospital."

Bertha hesitated and glanced at Paul again. "Oh, all right. Here." She handed the recipes to Sebastian.

"Thank you," said Sebastian. He carefully organized all the papers.

"I'm glad your water worked. It's tough to find good goalkeepers," Bertha said.

"Is that all of them?" asked Holly, fastening her eyes on Bertha.

"Why, of course," Bertha's eyes fluttered.

"Bertha," said her team, challenging her.

Bertha reached into her sleeve and pulled out a recipe.

"Here." She handed it over to Holly and she looked the other way.

CHAPTER SEVEN

Backward Pass

A few hours later, Paul Howard's hospital room looked like a flower shop. Roses, daisies, and flowers of every type and color filled the room.

"Who knew I had so many fans?" said Paul, admiring the garden-like scene around him. He lay on his bed wearing a white hospital gown with a white sheet pulled up to his chest.

"Well, you have three new fans right here," admitted Sebastian, nodding at Ralphy and Holly.

"We wanted to check up on you before we left," said Holly.

"Are you feeling better?" asked Ralphy. "That was some crash your head took—without a helmet."

"I... um... have a headache, and a huge bump on my noggin, but the doctor says I'll be fine." Paul said gently, while he removed the bag of ice from his head, felt the bump and winced.

"I want to thank you," said Sebastian. "We never would have been able to stay in the stadium and complete our mission if it wasn't for you."

"Ah, no problem. You just make sure Santa knows how good I've been."

Sebastian's eyes widened. "You know who we are?" said Sebastian.

"I may have smashed my head into a pole, but I'm not a dummy," replied Paul. "Let's just say you don't act like you're from around here." He paused. "And we should thank you. You helped inspire the team. I think we're going to have a real good year thanks to you."

Sebastian smiled. "You're wel-"

"Excuse me. May I come in?" It was Bertha. She noticed Sebastian, Holly and Ralphy. "Oh, it's the annoying goody two shoes elf people and the fur ball. I'll come back when you're gone." She started to back away.

"No," said Paul. "Come on in." He took a sip of his ginger ale.

Bertha hesitated and entered.

"I see you received my flowers. Looks like the florist read my book on floral arrangements. Very well done, I must say. And it should be, for the money I paid." Bertha plucked a flower and smelled it. "But you, Mr. Goalie, are worth it."

Paul spit out his ginger ale in a large spray. "*You* sent these to me?"

Bertha pushed Ralphy out of her way and walked toward Paul. "Yes. I felt badly for what happened to you."

Paul gripped his sheet and pulled it up higher to cover him.

"But what kind of klutz dives into a pole?" asked Bertha. She took Paul's glass of ginger ale from him and drank from his straw.

Ralphy and Holly flinched.

Paul quickly grabbed his drink back. "The kind that doesn't get paid enough, but still plays hard!" He adjusted the bag of ice on his head.

Bertha leaned in closer to Paul. "I pay you to block goals, not to leap into goal posts." She took the bag of ice from his head, opened it and began to scoop some fresh ice into it from an ice bucket on the nightstand next to him. "I played goalie a few times in college. I can help you with that." Bertha tried to place the ice bag gently on top of Paul's head.

Paul's face contorted. "Yeah, like *you* can teach me anything about goalkeeping. You stick to the kitchen. I bet I'm even a better cook than you."

"No way."

"Way."

"No way."

"Way."

"No way."

"Um. Excuse us, but we better be leaving," said Sebastian.

"Wait," said Holly. "I want to see who wins."

"Yeah," added Ralphy.

"I always win," said Bertha. She took the bag of ice and placed it on Paul's lap.

"Yow! Hey! That's cold!" shouted Paul. He scooped the bag off his lap.

"Sorry. They'll have to keep competing without us. We have to go home, but only after I get Mr. Howard's autograph." Sebastian picked up a pen from the nightstand.

"Sure! Just give me a piece of paper," grinned Paul. "I'll be happy to give you my autograph."

"Paper!" shouted Bertha. "Oh no! The newspaper!"

"What are you talking about?" asked Holly.

"I totally forgot about it! Really, I did!" said Bertha. "I had my assistant send the newspaper the secret location of Santa's workshop. If I know the *New York Gazette* it will be on the front page in the next edition!"

Sebastian, Ralphy and Holly stared at each other with blank faces.

"What should we do?" asked Ralphy.

"The right thing," said Paul. He placed his hand on Bertha's arm.

"No way, not again," said Bertha. "I already sacrificed those recipes." Bertha paused looking into Paul's blue eyes. She hesitated, then whipped out her cell phone from her pocket. "You're a bad influence, Goalie Boy. All right... I'll call the editor and see if I can stop it." She dialed. "I've been in the paper before, almost every other week actually. Maybe he'll listen to me."

Bertha waited for the editor to answer his phone. "Yes, hello, Perry, darling. Did you get the map I sent you? You did?" She was silent. "You plan on printing it right away. Oh, Perry, buddy, I'm calling to ask you not to do that. I should never have sent that to you. You see..." Bertha glanced at Paul. "I sent that when I wasn't in a good mood. It's just a silly map, please crumble it up and pretend I never sent it, as a favor to me." She paused again. "You won't do that? It's great news? It shows that I'm nuts! Let me tell you something—that paper of yours is a..." Bertha stopped her sentence. She felt Holly, Sebastian, Ralphy and Paul staring at her. "It's a fine paper. It would be better without that map though, and... I, I... wish you the best of everything."

Bertha hung up her phone. She placed her hand on her

head, feeling disoriented. "Looks like they're printing it." Bertha sat down on the side of the bed. She wiped her forehead. "Something's wrong. I feel strange. Normally, I feel great when something like this happens. But I actually feel kind of sick."

"I better call Santa," declared Holly, taking out her walkie talkie.

"That's your conscience, Bertha. I believe there's hope for you yet," said Sebastian. He placed his tiny hand in hers and handed her a box. "Here. This is an early Christmas gift from Santa and Mrs. Claus."

"A gift? For me?"

"Yep. Santa instructed us to give it to you before we left," said Sebastian.

Bertha opened the box. Her eyes shone with joy.

"We know you like candles. We hope you like it, and that it reminds you of the True Light of the world—the reason we celebrate Christmas." Sebastian winked at Paul.

"It's beautiful," said Bertha. "But... the Clauses are giving me a gift, even after everything I've done to them?"

"Yes. They forgive you and love you," said Sebastian.

Bertha was speechless and her eyes welled up with tears. She examined the candle more closely. "It's not wax. What's it made of?"

"That's another North Pole secret," said Sebastian cautiously.

"Um, excuse me," said Ralphy. "I hate to interrupt, but back to the newspaper problem... How many people read the *New York Gazette*?"

"Millions," answered Paul.

CHAPTER EIGHT
Kick Save!

As Chief of Security, Holly contacted Santa immediately on her walkie talkie. She explained how they had gotten the recipes back and how they now had a new emergency—Bertha had just remembered she had given the information about Santa's location to the newspaper. She even told Santa that Bertha seemed apologetic.

Santa and Mrs. Claus were relieved the recipes were safe. But now they faced a greater problem. In a matter of a day or two, thousands of curious individuals would discover their home and be knocking at their front door.

"Spalding! Please come to my office immediately!" Santa shouted into his intercom. Santa explained the situation, and moments later, Spalding arrived.

"We can't move our location that fast," admitted Spalding. "This is serious."

"If we have uninvited visitors we'll never get anything done around here." Santa said. He shook his head. "Our workshop must remain a secret!"

Spalding's mind shifted into high gear. "I must be alone

to think. The answer is there. I just have to ask the right questions."

"You've helped us out of every jam, Spalding," said Mrs. Claus. "We're counting on you."

Santa paused and shook his head sadly. "I don't believe I'm saying this, but I'm afraid this one just might be impossible."

Spalding turned on his heels and walked away in a trance.

"We don't have much time, Spalding!" Santa put his arm around Mrs. Claus and embraced her.

Meanwhile, back in New York City, Sebastian, Holly and Ralphy boarded the NickCruiser and flew North. Their long flight would take all night. All the way home, they each wondered what (and who) the next days would bring to the North Pole.

The next morning, the *New York Gazette* hit the newsstands with the following story:

Bertha the Soccer Star Claims to Discover Santa's Secret Workshop!

NEW YORK—It was just another day at the office for New York's "Queen" of cooking, crafting—and now soccer. Yesterday, Bertha Hayworth, the owner of the New York Blenders, proved her skills aren't limited to the kitchen or sewing machine. Bertha scored four goals and led her team to a 6 to 5 victory over the Norfolk Torpedoes, their first victory in two years.

The first woman ever to play in Pro-League Soccer, and someone never shy of publicity, Bertha also claimed yesterday

74

to have allegedly discovered the secret location of Santa's workshop.

"Her on-the-field antics and hand-drawn map revealing Santa's headquarters could be proof that Ms. Hayworth is finally in need of a long vacation, not headlines," said a source who wished to be unnamed.

The Commissioner of Pro-League Soccer has fined Ms. Hayworth $10,000 for breaking the league's rule, which states that "only men can play." She was also fined $1,000 for not playing in shorts.

Additionally, Blender goalkeeper Paul Howard was hospitalized after colliding headfirst into the goalpost while trying to make a save. The event marks the fifth time in Howard's career that he has smashed into the goalpost with his head.

Bertha's Map

Bertha Hayworth's hand-drawn map revealing the alleged secret location of Santa Claus's workshop. Source: Bertha Hayworth

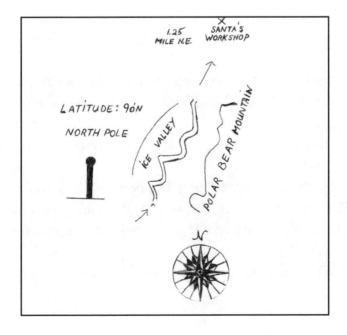

Back at the North Pole, Spalding laid on his bed, staring at the ceiling.

"We can't move the village," Spalding said out loud to himself. "We can't block the secret valley passage—it's too wide and the only way in or out. Unless someone comes in by use of flying reindeer, of course."

Meanwhile, in his office, Santa read the headline on the *Gazette's* Web site. He gazed at Bertha's hand drawn map below the article. "Oh dear, x marks the spot to... me," he said. He printed the page and showed the article to Mrs. Claus.

"Do you think anyone will take it seriously, dear?" asked Mrs. Claus. "It says Bertha needs a vacation. Maybe the world will think she's crazy."

"If even one person takes it seriously, we're in trouble," Santa replied. "They'll find us and tell everyone else." Santa clicked off his Internet access. "And it will only be a matter of hours before someone starts his journey North."

"Sorry we couldn't stop this."

Santa turned to see Holly. Her eyes were bloodshot from her long trip home with barely any sleep.

"Bertha really did feel bad about it," said Sebastian.

"I'm sure she did," said Santa. "But we still have to-"

Spalding entered the room. "Santa, I just don't know what to do. I've been thinking and thinking so hard my brain hurts."

"That's all right, Spalding. I've been thinking too and I can't come up with the answer. Maybe, we'll just have to accept it." Santa paused. "It was nice being a secret for all these years."

"Why can't we just hide?" said Sebastian, matter-of-factly.

Spalding took off his half-moon glasses. "What do you mean?"

"Like in hide and seek?" said Ralphy. "I love hide and seek!"

"No," said Sebastian. "We can hide our village."

Spalding put his glasses on.

"You can't hide an entire village, Sebastian!" cried Holly.

"Holly is right. What do you mean?" asked Santa.

"Why can't Spalding build a cloaking device that will hide our village from the human eye. If it works, we'll never have to worry about being located again."

"That's an interesting idea," said Spalding. "Using the laws of reflection, refraction and the speed of light, combined with the thin air here at the North Pole... Yes, I believe it can be done." Spalding flicked his suspenders like a guitar string.

"Then what are you standing here for? Make it so!" shouted Santa.

Sebastian smiled.

"Yes, sir!" Spalding spun around, ran out of the room, rushed into his laboratory and went to work.

Hours later, he had created seven machines designed to project and reflect light. He also made seven large mirrors.

It was now time to test Spalding's invention.

All the elves, Ralphy, Santa and Mrs. Claus stood anxiously outside near the perimeter of Santa's village waiting to see if it would work. The polar bears guarded the area from their security posts. The elves had helped Spalding position the mirrors and projection machines at the proper strategic locations around the village. They were still setting up, when suddenly, they heard dogs barking in the distance.

"Oh no! What's that?" said Sebastian.

Holly picked up her super-powered telescope. "Looks like it's our first unwanted explorer. It's a man with a dogsled team. Hurry, Spalding!"

Spalding rushed to make some final connections with wires.

"May I see?" asked Ralphy.

Holly handed him the telescope.

Ralphy focused the device. "Hey, I… I think I know that guy!"

"Who is it?" asked Sebastian, taking the telescope from Ralphy. "Oh no! Spalding, hurry!"

Spalding frantically connected more wires.

"I'd recognize that nose anywhere!" Sebastian peered through the telescope.

"Who is it?" asked Santa.

Sebastian took the telescope away from his eye and fastened his eyes on Santa. "It's the Boca Elks football coach—Bud Hill. And he's holding the *New York Gazette!*"

"He's here to take the polar bears away to play on his team!" said Holly.

Sebastian looked through the telescope again. He saw Coach Bud Hill alone on a sleigh pulled by eight dogs. He was getting closer.

"He's coming down the valley and heading right for us," said Sebastian. "He must see the workshop!"

"I'm engaging the unit now!" Spalding flicked a switch on a black box.

In the distance, Coach Hill stopped the sleigh. "Whoa! Doggies!" He dropped his reins, stepped off the sleigh, and stared at Santa's workshop. "Ho ho ho! This is my lucky day. Hello polar bears and my NFL championship!" Coach Hill took off his mittens, opened his duffel bag, and took out a camera.

Sebastian turned to Santa. "We must not be invisible! He's getting a camera! He's going to take a picture of us! Hurry, Spalding! Do something!"
Spalding wildly checked the cable connections. "It should be working!"

Coach Hill pulled the camera out of its protective case. "Impressive workshop, Mr. Claus."

Sebastian's face grew angry. "Why can't these people just leave us alone?" Sebastian kicked Spalding's black box.

Suddenly, the entire village disappeared in front of the coach's eyes. Coach Hill shook his head violently, like a wet dog drying off. "What happened?" He rubbed his eyes. "Where did it go?"

Holly took the telescope from Sebastian and aimed it at Coach Hill. "He put the camera down! He's not taking the picture! I think it's working!"

Coach Hill squinted ahead, looking closely for anything. All he could see was snow and ice. "Huh. Must have been another mirage," he said, softly to himself. Coach Hill glanced at the Bertha's Fancy Fruitcake on his sled. "That disgusting Bertha Fruitcake must be making me see things. That stuff isn't fit for a dog," he told his hounds. They barked in return.

Inside the perimeter of Santa's village, everyone cheered and shook Spalding's hand.

"Great job, Spalding! You did it!" shouted Holly.

Spalding smiled proudly.

Sebastian jumped up and down on one leg. "Ouch! Ouch! Ouch! I hurt my big toe!"

"You should have kicked it with the inside of your foot like a soccer player!" said Ralphy.

Sebastian gave Ralphy a look.

Coach Bud Hill turned his sleigh around. He looked at the map on the newspaper and at the snow mountain to his right. "There's Polar Bear Mountain. Here's the valley. The Workshop should be right there." He crumbled up the front page of the *New York Gazette* and threw it as hard as he could into the wind. The paper caught in a wind drift and sailed away. "That crazy BERTHA!" the coach shouted.

Bertha's name echoed throughout the valley.

Mrs. Claus hugged her husband. "Looks like we don't have to worry about unwanted visitors anymore."

"That's great news," said Santa. "Maybe now we can get back to our mission—making toys and cookies."

"You know, I think saving Christmas and soccer have a lot in common," said Holly.

"How so?" asked Santa, curiously.

"They're both a real *kick* sometimes."

"You can say that again," said Sebastian, nursing his sore big toe.

"I was wrong," added Ralphy. "I guess elves can kick after all."

THE END

80

Post Game Report

This post game report is brought to you by Bertha's Bagels, the best tasting bagels in New York City.

Dear Reader:

The New York Blenders had a great season and won their first championship. The team also made money for the first time, which Bertha decided to invest back into the soccer team. Paul Howard led the league in saves and shutouts—and didn't crash his head into the goalpost at all during the rest of the season.

Bertha Hayworth sold her other businesses and focused on her first love—soccer. She challenged the commissioner's ruling that only men could play in the league and won—she played in every game for the remainder of the season. Bertha broke all scoring and assist records—and became the team's Most Valuable Player!

Paul Howard and Bertha Hayworth became close friends. Many of Paul's teammates wondered if this was the result of too many collisions with goalposts, but they never said anything to him. Paul saw that, deep down (way deep down) Bertha was good and the two now plan to open a chain of soccer-themed restaurants where they both will create the recipes and do the cooking.

Bertha discovered that, when people cheat, they lose an opportunity to do their very best. She also found out that it is hard to change one of the consequences of stealing and cheating—a bad reputation. Bertha is trying hard to restore her good name by doing good deeds and by being totally honest.

Bertha loved her candle and sent Santa and Mrs. Claus the following thank you letter:

My dearest Mrs. Claus (a lovely and talented woman) and Santa,

Thank you for the wonderful candle. It burns bright and has a scent that warms the spirit. Remarkable! At first I wondered how you knew I loved candles, but then I remembered that you are the Clauses after all, and if you know when I am good and bad then you must know I love candles too. I love lots of thing actually, I don't have enough monogrammed stationery to name them all, but now I sense that I am starting to like things less and people more. Back to the candle, I am still curious what it is made of. My research and development team cannot figure it out either. Any hints? I know it is a North Pole secret and I'll accept that.

I also want to send my sincerest apologies for all the pain I caused you and your elves (they are as cute as they are small!). To show my appreciation for your kindness and in hopes that this forgiveness circle will now be complete, I am enclosing a copy (hot off the presses) of my new book on Christmas decorating entitled *Bertha's Dreaming of a North Pole Christmas.*

I hope you will delight in the many images of Christmas décor within its glossy pages and perfectly bound cover. And I must too also apologize if these room designs remotely resemble anything at your humble home. My company lawyer has promised me that I need not worry about any potential lawsuit from you because you do not exist, but you and I know better. I'm confident that the Christmas spirit will reign in your hearts and that you are too loving and busy to deal with matters of the court.

I must be going now. Big plans and so little time.

Lotion and lotions of love always,

Bertha Hayworth

P.S.

It is my goal that you only will hear good things about me from now on—and you know how seriously I take my goals, pun intended.

I heard that upon reading the letter that Mrs. Claus immediately opened the book and discovered that Bertha's interior designs looked just like the rooms within Santa's workshop. Mrs. Claus then remembered the empty film canister she found with Bertha's note. She decided that, she too, should go into the decorating business.

Santa pleaded with her "Let's just stick to toy building, please."

To which Mrs. Claus replied, "Maybe Bertha and I should become a team?"

The comment caused Santa to roll his eyes.

Bertha also sent everyone at the North Pole a special Christmas gift—a frame with her photograph in it. Sebastian keeps the photo under his bed where it scares Ralphy when he hides there during games of hide and seek.

I hope you enjoyed *Elves Can't Kick!*

Keep kicking and have a wonderful Christmas!

Robert Skead

Join the Sports Adventurers Club!
For Elves Can't Dunk, Tackle and Kick Fans

Visit www.robertskead.com and discover how you can become an official team member of the Sports Adventurers Club and receive your own certificate that you can display!

Be part of the team!

Life is good. Sports are Fun. Adventures are exciting.